BANANAS IN PYJAMAS

Nursery Rhymes

Compiled by

SIMON HOPKINSON

Illustrated by

PAUL PATTIE

Contents

THE MULBERRY BUSH 4

OLD MACDONALD 7

LITTLE BO-PEEP 9

PAT-A-CAKE 10

HUMPTY DUMPTY 11

BAA, BAA, BLACK SHEEP 12

MARY HAD A LITTLE LAMB 12

THE LITTLE NUT-TREE 14

LADYBIRD, LADYBIRD 15

SEE-SAW, MARGERY DAW 16

POP GOES THE WEASEL 17

MARY, MARY 18

LITTLE MISS MUFFET 19

OLD KING COLE 20

HEY DIDDLE DIDDLE 21

IT'S RAINING 22

INCY WINCY 22

HICKORY DICKORY DOCK 24

JACK AND JILL 25

SING A SONG OF SIXPENCE 27

MISS POLLY 28

RING-A-RING O'ROSES 29

TWINKLE, TWINKLE 31

THE MULBERRY BUSH

Here we go round the mulberry bush,
the mulberry bush, the mulberry bush,
Here we go round the mulberry bush,
So early in the morning!

This is the way we wash our face,
wash our face, wash our face,
This is the way we wash our face,
So early in the morning!

This is the way we comb our hair,
comb our hair, comb our hair,
This is the way we comb our hair,
So early in the morning!

This is the way we brush our teeth,
brush our teeth, brush our teeth,
This is the way we brush our teeth,
So early in the morning!

OLD MACDONALD

Old Macdonald had a farm, E I E I O,

And on that farm he had some cows, E I E I O.

With a moo, moo here, and a moo, moo there,

Here a moo, there a moo, everywhere a moo, moo.

Old Macdonald had a farm, E I E I O.

Old Macdonald had a farm, E I E I O,

And on that farm he had some ducks, E I E I O.

With a quack, quack here, and a quack, quack there...

Old Macdonald had a farm, E I E I O,

And on that farm he had some dogs, E I E I O.

With a woof, woof here, and a woof, woof there...

Old Macdonald had a farm, E I E I O,

And on that farm he had some sheep, E I E I O.

With a baa, baa here, and a baa, baa there...

Old Macdonald had a farm, E I E I O,

And on that farm he had some pigs, E I E I O.

With an oink, oink here, and an oink, oink there,

Here an oink, there an oink, everywhere an oink, oink.

Old Macdonald had a farm, E I E I O.

LITTLE BO-PEEP

Little Bo-peep has lost her sheep,
And doesn't know where to find them;
Leave them alone, and they'll come home,
Wagging their tails behind them.

PAT-A-CAKE

Pat-a-cake, pat-a-cake, baker's man,

Bake me a cake as fast as you can;

Pat it and prick it, and mark it with B,

And put it in the oven for Bananas and me!

HUMPTY DUMPTY

Humpty Dumpty sat on a wall.

Humpty Dumpty had a great fall;

All the King's horses and all the King's men,

Couldn't put Humpty together again.

BAA, BAA, BLACK SHEEP

Baa, baa, black sheep, Have you any wool?

Yes, sir, yes, sir. Three bags full;

One for the master, And one for the dame,

And one for the little boy who lives down the lane.

MARY HAD A LITTLE LAMB

Mary had a little lamb,

Its fleece was white as snow;

And everywhere that Mary went,

The lamb was sure to go.

It followed her to school one day,

That was against the rule;

It made the children laugh and play,

To see a lamb at school.

THE LITTLE NUT-TREE

I had a little nut-tree,

Nothing would it bear

But a silver nutmeg

And a golden pear.

The King of Spain's daughter

Came to visit me,

All for the sake

Of my little nut-tree.

LADYBIRD, LADYBIRD

Ladybird, ladybird,

Fly away home,

Your house is on fire

And your children all gone;

All except one,

And that's little Ann,

And she has crept under

The frying pan.

SEE-SAW, MARGERY DAW

See-saw, Margery Daw,

Johnny shall have a new master;

He shall have but a penny a day,

Because he can't work any faster.

POP GOES THE WEASEL

Half a pound of tuppeny rice,

Half a pound of treacle,

Mix it up and make it nice,

Pop goes the weasel.

MARY, MARY

Mary, Mary, quite contrary,

How does your garden grow?

With silver bells and cockle shells,

And pretty maids all in a row.

LITTLE MISS MUFFET

Little Miss Muffet sat on a tuffet,

Eating her curds and whey;

There came a big spider, who sat down beside her

And frightened Miss Muffet away.

OLD KING COLE

Old King Cole was a merry old soul,
And a merry old soul was he;
He called for his pipe and he called for his bowl,
And he called for his fiddlers three.

HEY DIDDLE DIDDLE

Hey diddle diddle,

The cat and the fiddle,

The cow jumped over the moon;

The little dog laughed

To see such sport

And the dish ran away with the spoon.

IT'S RAINING

It's raining, it's pouring,

The old man is snoring;

He went to bed

And bumped his head

And couldn't get up in the morning.

INCY WINCY

Incy Wincy spider

Climbing up the spout;

Down came the rain

And washed poor Incy out.

Out came the sun

And dried up all the rain;

So Incy Wincy spider

Climbed up the spout again.

HICKORY DICKORY DOCK

Hickory dickory dock,

The mouse ran up the clock.

The clock struck one,

The mouse ran down,

Hickory dickory dock.

JACK AND JILL

Jack and Jill went up the hill,
To fetch a pail of water;
Jack fell down and broke his crown,
And Jill came tumbling after.

Then up Jack got and home did trot,
As fast as he could caper;
He went to bed and patched his head
With vinegar and brown paper.

SING A SONG OF SIXPENCE

Sing a song of sixpence

A pocket full of rye;

Four and twenty blackbirds,

Baked in a pie.

When the pie was opened,

The birds began to sing;

Now wasn't that a dainty dish,

To set before the king?

The king was in his counting-house,

Counting out his money;

The queen was in the parlour,

Eating bread and honey.

The maid was in the garden,

Hanging out the clothes,

When down came a blackbird

And pecked off her nose.

MISS POLLY

Miss Polly had a dolly who was sick, sick, sick,

So she phoned for the doctor to come quick, quick, quick!

The doctor came with her bag and her hat,

And she knocked on the door with a rat-tat-tat!

She looked at the dolly and she shook her head,

Then she said, 'Miss Polly, put her straight to bed.'

She wrote on a pad for a pill, pill, pill.

' I'll be back in the morning with my bill, bill, bill.'

RING-A-RING O' ROSES

Ring-a-ring o' roses,

A pocket full of posies,

A-tishoo! A-tishoo!

We all fall down.

The cows are in the meadow,

Eating buttercups,

A-tishoo! A-tishoo!

We all jump up!

TWINKLE, TWINKLE

Twinkle, twinkle, little star.
How I wonder what you are!
Up above the world so high,
Like a diamond in the sky.
Twinkle, twinkle, little star,
How I wonder what you are!

Published by ABC Books for the
AUSTRALIAN BROADCASTING CORPORATION
GPO Box 9994 Sydney NSW 2001

Copyright © Bananas in Pyjamas Australian Broadcasting Corporation

Copyright © compilation Harvest Lane Pty Ltd 1997

Copyright © illustrations Paul Pattie 1997

Original song by Carey Blyton

First published 1997

Reprinted December 1997

Reprinted April 1998

First paperback edition May 1999

All rights reserved. No part of this publication may be reproduced, stored in a retrieval system or transmitted in any form or by any means electronic, mechanical, photocopying, recording or otherwise, without the prior written permission of the Australian Broadcasting Corporation.

National Library of Australia
Cataloguing-in-Publication entry
Hopkinson, Simon,1947— .
Bananas in pyjamas: nursery rhymes.
ISBN 0 7333 0599 7. Hardback
ISBN 0 7333 0802 3. Paperback
1.Nursery rhymes I. Pattie, Paul. II. Australian Broadcasting Corporation.
III. Title. IV. Title: Bananas in pyjamas (Television program).
398.8

This publication was produced in co-operation with
ABC Children's Television.
Bronwyn Morgan for ABC TV.
The illustrations were painted with coloured inks.
Set in Pelham
Designed and typeset by Monkeyfish
Colour separations by First Media, Adelaide
Printed in Singapore by Tien Wah Press

2 4 5 3 1